For Poppy and Leo – J.D.

For Lou Bass – K.G.

First published 2013 by Macmillan Children's Books
This edition published 2018 by Macmillan Children's Books
an imprint of Pan Macmillan
20 New Wharf Road, London N1 9RR
Associated companies throughout the world
www.panmacmillan.com

ISBN: 978-1-5290-0597-4

1 3 5 7 9 8 6 4 2

A CIP catalogue record for this book is available from the British Library.

Printed in China

Wake Up Do, Lydia Lou!

Julia Donaldson

Illustrated by Karen George

MACMILLAN CHILDREN'S BOOKS

One night a
ghost glided
into Lydia
Lou's bedroom
when she was
fast asleep.

The ghost said: WHOO!
Wake up do, Lydia Lou!
Wake up from your dream
And scream!

4

But Lydia Lou didn't wake up.

The ghost tried again.
This time he jumped out and said:

BOO!
WHOO!

Wake up do, Lydia Lou!
Wake from your dream
And scream!

6

But Lydia Lou went on sleeping.

"I need some help," said the ghost.
So he fetched a kitten.

MEW!
BOO!
WHOO!

Wake up do, Lydia Lou!
Wake from your dream
And scream!

But Lydia Lou just smiled in her sleep.

"I need some more help," said the ghost.
So he fetched a cow.

MOO!
MEW!

BOO!
WHOO!
Wake up do, Lydia Lou!
Wake from your dream
And scream!

Lydia Lou turned onto her
back and began to snore.

"I need some more help," said the ghost.
So he fetched an owl.
TOO-WHIT-TOO-WHOO!
MOO!
MEW!

BOO!
WHOO!
Wake up do, Lydia Lou!
Wake from your dream
And scream!

But Lydia Lou just
hugged her teddy a bit
tighter.

"I need some more help," said the ghost.
So he fetched a baby.

BOO HOO!
TOO-WHIT-TOO-WHOO!
MOO!
MEW!

The teddy looked a tiny bit scared, but Lydia Lou just kept on sleeping.

BOO!
WHOO!

Wake up do, Lydia Lou!
Wake from your dream
And scream!

"I need some more help," said the ghost.
So he fetched a cockerel.

COCK-A-DOODLE-DOO!
BOO HOO!
TOO-WHIT-TOO-WHOO!
MOO!
MEW!

BOO!
WHOO!
Wake up do, Lydia Lou!
Wake from your dream
And scream!

Lydia Lou slept on, and
a feather floated out of
her pillow.

The feather tickled the ghost's nose

It tickled the cow's nose,

And it tickled the beaks of the birds.

and the kitten's nose.

and the baby's nose too.

All together, they let out an enormous sneeze . . .

A-a-aaa-choooo!

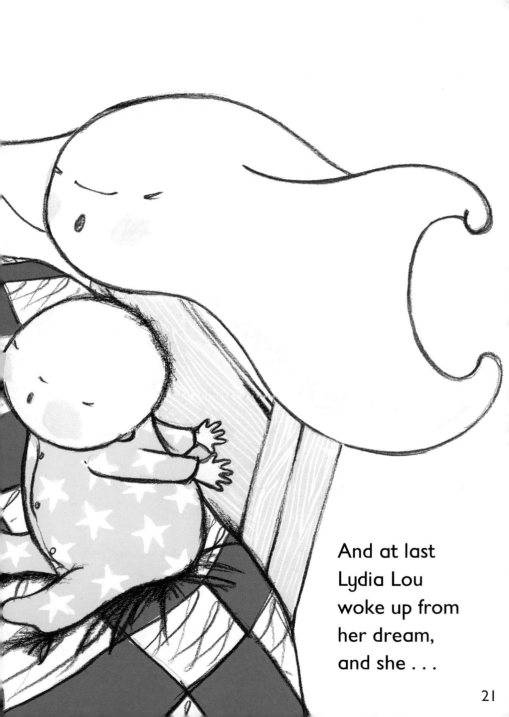

And at last
Lydia Lou
woke up from
her dream,
and she . . .

. . . laughed!